All Things Danish

A Novella

Frank G. Merlino

for Debra,

as always

Italian for Beginners

First of all, I think it is important to clear up right away that the Danish are not Dutch. The Dutch live in Netherlands, sometimes called Holland and their capital city is Amsterdam. The Danes live in Denmark, always called Denmark and their capital city is Copenhagen.

I am not exactly sure why I decided to go all Danish all the time, but it may be due to my losing my job a few months ago.

I mean I am not Danish. I have never been to Denmark and certainly do not speak Danish. I have had Danishes at breakfast.

I think I was just looking for something. I wanted to belong to something. It was not going to be my old company or career anymore as they sacked me pretty unceremoniously, I thought, for having put in so many years. They just herded a few hundred of us into the corporate auditorium one day and said see you later.

What happened to building a career and sacrificing marriage and kids so as to try and break the glass ceiling? I had devoted several years of my life working as an actuarial for one of the biggest insurance companies in the world.

I wallowed in my shock, anger, sadness and then slowly began to accept that I am single, unemployed and nearing forty. While wallowing I realized there are two kinds of pain and both make you feel bad inside. Pain that you feel from guilt when you hurt others and pain that you feel when others have hurt you. I have felt both it just happens that this time the pain was inflicted on me by others.

That first morning waking up with no place you have to be was the toughest. It was still my body, but I felt different inside it. That morning in the kitchen making coffee as I had always done first thing even felt different. It was the same coffee maker, but I was different. I was unemployed. I was making coffee as an unemployed person. This went on for many days, familiar objects but a different me. I considered each action very intentionally as if doing it for the first time since I actually had time to really think about what it is I was doing. Nothing became automatic.

So why not just become Danish? They seem cool. I could learn the language and save my money, once I get some again and then dream of all dreams go there. Plus, I would make myself feel good again by doing good. Do good. Feel good. Feel good. Do good.

So please now refer to me now as Maggie Gindale. Dane. Why not? I had no say in picking my parents, my gender, my ethnicity or where I was born. Now that I am free to chose a different me, why not pick what I want to be? I am reborn. You think about how random your life is. Even when I had a say in my life my choices were equally random. The first important choice I made was college and then I just went where my friends were going. My job was the result of the first company to offer me one at the campus job fair. My first serious love affair was with my boss. How original was that? He was simply there, came onto me and the combination of his worldliness and the vague notion in my mind that it might also help my career propelled me into his life. I am not proud of those feelings, like I said, I have hurt people. I guess you could say I took advantage of him. He was older and really did not want a long term relationship and it eventually went nowhere. We both ended up with what we deserved. Nothing. Now it is all these years later and I commit to be more intentional with my life. I am going to try to do things for the right reason whether it is a big thing or just a small everyday thing.

So my layoff was really a good thing. As Joseph Campbell the anthropologist and expert on cultures used to say and I paraphrase, sometimes you discover as you are going up the ladder that it is up against the wrong wall. It is great. I now fill my days when I am not looking for work with listening to Danish language tapes, studying travel books on Denmark and watching Danish films which are not as easy to get as one might think.

I started with the film, *Italian for Beginners*, which though it has an odd title is in Danish and made in Denmark and though the plot centers on Danes trying to learn to speak Italian, I focused on listening to the Danish language and studying the subtitles and tried to ignore the Italian. The film was perfect for me because it was basically about six lonely singles in their 30s looking for something to do. It was directed by Danish filmmaker Lone Scherfig. According to Scherfig,

> "It's just a film about having no one to have pasta with and having someone to have pasta with."

It was a miracle I found the film. One day as I had just finished job searching on Career Builders I decided to give myself a break and went to the local Blockbusters.

It was going out of business and had everything in big bins all piled high and on sale. I asked the attendant about Danish films. He fought back a yawn and pointed me towards a bin labeled in magic marker, "Foregn" - yes misspelled, but I guess they were in a hurry to move their inventory. I dug around, but thought I had found nothing, but I bought *Italian for Beginners* anyway thinking at least I found a foreign film and many people have said they love Italy and plus I did not want to go home empty handed to an empty apartment and an empty afternoon. So I got it home, drew the shades and made my apartment especially dark for the early afternoon, the rainy day helped too and made some popcorn and settled in, not even looking at the movie description on the cover, then amazingly there was that beautiful clipped Danish language. I thought this is surely a sign. I am destined to go to Denmark.

Carlsberg

I remember one night while lying in bed a few days after watching *Italian for Beginners*, I had a thought and it made me sit bolt upright and write myself a note for the morning. You know how sometimes you are thinking and things that seem unrelated just kinda lead to each other as if your brain synapses had brushed against each other in unexpected ways and put odd thoughts next to each other.

Yes, beer, not that I like it, but I remembered reading an antidote in a physics text during college that Niels Bohr, famous for quantum physics and Danish loved beer so much that he had his local brewery, Carlsberg, put a tap directly to his home in Copenhagen. Note to me, "find Carlsberg" which turned out not so easy to do. It is not carried at just any grocery store or convenience store. I found it at a specialty liquor store that had imported beers. I got a nice look from the young cashier as he looked me up and down. I assumed he thought, *nice choice in brew lady*.

So that afternoon, I found my old physics book from Lewis and Clark University and clipped out the picture of

Niels Bohr and tacked it to my bulletin board above my computer and popped open a cold one. The bottle is a beautiful green with a small label around the neck that says, "by appointment of the Danish Monarchy, Copenhagen, Denmark". I take the first drink and consider what a great thing it is to be able to swallow a piece of Copenhagen, Denmark while sitting here in Portland. One has to be impressed with world commerce and its speed. Last night I thought of Carlsberg. Today I drink Carlsberg. I drank while reading the travel book on Copenhagen I had bought before coming home. I am starting to like beer more, maybe because it is Danish now.

I have continued my secret affair with Niels and at five o'clock each day, Niels and I share happy hour together with a Carlsberg.

Meanwhile, the job hunting goes slowly. I go to interviews, try and say what I think they want to hear and then end the visit with that awkward realization among us that, *this really isn't what any of us want is it?"*

I have a support group of friends who either have been or are also unemployed and when we get together I accept the sympathy and well wishes head on and hope to move onto other subjects.

Many are amazed a female, forty or older and Asian could get laid off in this day and age of affirmative action. Some have encouraged me to sue or go to the EEOC, but that is not the way of the Asian culture. My parents hid their pain. They taught me an aggressiveness in achievement, but not at the expense of others. Besides, my friends do not know that my old boss was married when I had the affair with him and his friends at the company in influential places may have held it against me. I am glad in this instance my parents are not around to know this fact either. It is not anything I am proud of or can prove.

After interviews, I often return to my apartment and do the things you do when you have time like this, go through and discard expired grocery coupons, clean underneath the cabinet below the kitchen sink and vacuuming things you had not noticed before had collected food crumbs.

I became in tune with my apartment complex's daily rhythms like when the mailman arrives or the garbage dumpster is emptied. I also noticed that a hush descends on the neighborhood at nine as the commuters have left for work, kids are in school and the day is left to those of us with nowhere to have to be, not all of us of the retired set or stay home Moms. So we jog, bike or walk, nodding knowingly to each other and imagining when that call for an interview might come. We look on as the cable line repairmen do their work and think, it must be great to have a job. There is the city employee on his riding mower mowing the grass in the fields and traffic islands, cutting into nature to provide that smell of life and hope. A wave to the school crossing guard, packing up for the day and on their way home.

One bad moment came as I was jogging past the strip mall whose anchor store had been the Blockbuster where I had found *Italian for Beginners* at, the space now empty. For some reason I stopped. I never stop while jogging. But I did then and unexpectedly started to cry and all the tears that had been saved from being strong and proactive came rushing out. A temporary banner hung that said, "Halloween Store Coming Soon," but I knew this to be just temporary and then it would be gone after October 31. So I cried for all the former employees of the anchor store. I cried for the temporary employees of the Halloween Store that would have to find another job in November. I cried for those who had been laid off with me in that auditorium that made us feel like we were being herded. I cried for a bygone era where professionals or college types thought they might avoid job loss. I cried for parents who are told the news and wish they could protect their children from what they have themselves been through. I cried for all my wonderful friends who are mad for me.

My savings are hanging in there as I have really watched my costs since there is no family or friends to fall back on. I walk or ride my bike whenever possible so as to save on gas. I eat pretty frugally. I have found that saving money can also be entertaining and a good way to kill time, example, the coin processing machine at the bank. Bring your Mason jars full of coins and pour them in. Watch it turn them on a spinning platform and spit out a receipt. Except for my splurges on Carlsberg, language tapes, travel books and films, I really do not spend much. I think I am doing pretty good overall and I have a nice healthy hobby, becoming Danish plus a great imaginary friend, Niels Bohr. He has two middle names, Henrik and David and was born October 7, 1885. It is a May/December romance. He won the Nobel Prize in 1922, you know. I will not even go into how he had it all over Einstein when it came to understanding the universe and natural world.

A Google search informed me the two other most famous Danes are Soren Kierkegaard and Hans Christian Anderson. I am sticking with Niels as my fantasy boyfriend.

Skibsted Bikes

I read in my travel book on Copenhagen that Danes love their bikes and bike almost everywhere and are very environmental in this way. Now when I ride my bike to the grocers or cleaners to save on gas, even though I have a Prius it is still expensive, I just pretend I am in Copenhagen. The Danes best bike designer is Jens Martin Skibsted or at least that is what was said on the Travel channel when they were doing a feature on Copenhagen being the most bike friendly city in the world and listed Portland here as being the most bike friendly in the United States. I was just channel surfing one afternoon and came upon the program, believe it or not. I think it is amazing how information seems to find you when you are focused on a topic. Jens is quite attractive and had some brilliant ideas and ways of thinking about urban planning and design. My heart though belongs to Niels at the moment. As I think of it now, I do not think I have ever met a Dane in person.

I have made it to the cleaners with my clothes in the bag they provide. I can throw the bag over my shoulder when I ride as it has a shoulder strap. This is especially handy when I need to make any sudden stops and need both hands on the handle bars like at traffic lights I misjudge.

I give my clothes to Mr. Woo as I always do. He seems to always be here running the store. Occasionally I see his wife and daughters in back. He has introduced me to them at one time or another. I considered stopping my dry cleaning due to costs, but then realized that for interviews, I needed to look my best and I just cannot iron a blouse as well as Mr. Woo can dry clean and starch it. I tried for a couple weeks using spray starch, but always felt a loss of confidence at interviews fearing my collar was being stared at for being creased. I have cut back on taking to the dry cleaners anything that will not be worn for an interview, so that has helped with some dry cleaning cost.

I am happy to be. Some may look at my life and say, boy you must really be depressed or it must be rough, and that was the case at first, but now I am enjoying each moment. Maybe I am deluding myself, but there are far worse things and I still have plenty of choices and am still doing what I want each day.

At night as I lay in bed before falling asleep I evaluate how my day went. I judge myself now by my own standards. I think I am basically a good person. I no longer judge my day based on what my boss thought, of course he is gone now anyway or what my significant other thinks, of course not that there is one at the moment. I know my value. I am not saying this is easy. My thoughts often get crowded by worries about *what is so and so thinking of me* and I replay the words and actions of others from the day, but mostly I try to block this all out now and return to, *what do I think*?

Skagen Watches

My new career as a "private eye" evolved by accident and not very consciously, despite my best efforts to control my choices, I still just sort of evolve into things. I guess "private eye" might be giving my first job since my layoff a little too much glamour.

Mr. Woo was telling me a few days ago about his nephew Dang who was supposed to visit him from China and has still not shown up. The whole family is worried. He said, "Dang no come. You smart. You help."

"But what can I do, Mr. Woo? This is a job for the police or the customs officials."

"We try them. They know nothing. No help. No care. You help. I pay you."

Mr. Woo gave me my dry cleaning and an envelope. The envelope had $100 in it. Thinking back on it now I guess he was desperate and knowing I was a college graduate and had a good job at a big insurance company, I do not think I had mentioned to him about my unemployment, he thought I might know something or someone. I also think since I looked liked one of his daughters he trusted me.

The first thing I thought to do was ask him for the number of his nephew's parents so that I could ask them a few questions like, did he get on the plane? Did he call during any layover or plane changes? Mr. Woo had trouble understanding what I wanted so his daughter, the one I look like, came from the backroom and gave me the number. She explained that her cousin Dang, according to his parents had boarded his flight. However, he was not on it when she and her father had gone to meet him at the Portland airport. They had registered him as a missing person before leaving the airport and had since spoken to various authorities. We chatted a bit more. She explained their family had come from China by way of Seattle before settling on Portland. As I left Woo Cleaners, I worried how I was going to make a call to China and did I remember my Cantonese well enough to speak to Dang's parents in Canton. I was learning Danish, but might have to brush up on Cantonese before long.

My other P.I. assignment is the one that has me heading to Kate's Espresso and Yoga to put up a few flyers. My neighbor, Mrs. Grandholm has lost her Terrier, Terry and asked for my help. I have not been paid yet, but the reward is $50 and so I have hope. I guess you could say I have two clients. Mr. Woo and Mrs. Grandholm. I have to be careful not to spend the money in my mind too soon before I even have earned it. I saw a Danish watch brand called Skagen while surfing the net. It is beautiful. I will have to report any earnings to my unemployment office so I still better be careful about purchases.

Armed with flyers that have a picture of Terry and contact information and a handful of push pins I am careful to avoid sticking myself with, I enter the coffee aroma atmosphere of Kate's. Kate's is just a couple blocks from my apartment so I did not even have to ride my bike. Kate's a friend from college who runs, you guessed it, a coffee house combined with a yoga studio.

This is my favorite corner of my neighborhood as there is a vegetarian co-op, Powell's Books and an Apple store. All have cork bulletin boards that the community can use to post information, except the Apple store which is really new and slick. I spend a lot of time on this corner looking at books in Powell's, looking at the latest by Apple or eating ice cream at the co-op. They make it themselves and have the most remarkable flavors with the funniest names. My favorite is called "Elvis, the Fat Years," really. Others I really like are Chocolate Smoked Sea Salt, Szechuan Strawberry and Cucumber Ice Milk.

I stick a flyer of Terry, his sad brown eyes starring right at me as if he were trying to tell me where he was at, next to the flyer on a new class in movement and martial arts starting next week. There is a picture of a Ninja warrior on it and so it might help get Terry some attention by being next to it.

I had already walked my block looking for Terry, knocking on each door and leaving the flyer. I was amazed at how many neighbors I had not met before or even seen. I was also amazed at how often I had to knock on some doors before someone was home or answered, going to one home on four different occasions at different times of the day before a middle aged man answered and while scratching his belly said he remembered seeing Terry in the alley behind his house but did not remember seeing him with a collar or tags.

"Did you see him in the alley after the 27th, that is when he went missing from his owner or had you seen him there before?"

"I can't remember if it was before or after, but it was only once."

"Do you remember what he was doing?"

He seemed to find this funny and said, "he's a dog, he was sniffing around, what do you think he was doing?"

I thanked him for his time and left a little embarrassed as I walked down the steps from his front door as I was leaving, but I thought it was a good question. If he had been fighting with another dog I would then know he might be hurt, just as an example. My first lead had not been much to go on as Terry was not in the alley when I went there. However, Mrs. Grandholm had said Terry had a collar and tags. That was the first question I had asked her and she assured me he did. Was the belly scratcher mistaken?

Hamlet was a Dane

I was getting a bit of cabin fever being in my apartment so much and walking or riding my bike in the neighborhood when the idea for a road trip hit me.

I was at Powell's window shopping for books when I picked up a free community paper near the exit as I was leaving. I stuck it in my bag and headed to Alberta street on my bike so as to have a late breakfast at the Tin Shed, my favorite is their salmon omelets.

. Once my salmon omelet arrived, I pulled out the community paper and flipped through while eating. I normally did this and am not bothered by eating alone in a public place. As I flipped through it I made a note to call about how much it might cost to place an add in it regarding Terry. Then it hit me. I was looking at this years line-up of plays at the Oregon Shakespeare Festival in Ashland and saw that they were doing *Hamlet* in honor of their 75th season. Hamlet was a Dane. I must go see *Hamlet*. I had tortured through reading the play in high school, but had never seen it performed.

I biked home as soon as I could and hit Google. It was 297 miles to Ashland from Portland heading south. I would have to drive and it was going to take me about five hours. I could sleep in my car after the play and then drive back the next morning. I ordered the cheapest ticket available, only $10 for what they described on-line as a "lawn seat" for pick-up at Will Call tomorrow night. I would leave first thing in the morning. This was the best thing about not having a job, I had no schedule tomorrow, until now.

I began packing. I put in a duffel toiletries, a change of clothing, my Columbia all purpose wind breaker in case it rained which was a possibility every day. I packed my Danish language tapes to listen to during the drive and made extra coffee for a thermos to take with me.

While in bed tonight I calculate how much the trip will cost with gas and decide to save money by tomorrow morning packing a lunch and dinner and then breakfast, so I never have to eat out while there. I make a mental note to swing by Powell's in the morning before leaving the city to get a used copy of *Hamlet*.

I felt ready and fell asleep. I had set my alarm for the exact time of sunrise, according to the weather web site, so as to make the most of the next day.

I bounced out of bed and turned the alarm off. I showered, dressed, made sure to unplug the blender after making a wheat germ smoothie for breakfast and was out the door. I was heading under the highway sign that said Ashland bright and early, even with my stops for gas and Powell's.

I drove straight through stopping only once for gas and a break in Eugene which was almost the half way point. I ate my lunch as I drove and listened to either my Danish language CDs or Copenhagen radio on my Sirius satellite receiver, my last fun impulse buy before my layoff.

The drive filled me with life as I saw the Rouge River Valley and the Siskiyou and Cascade mountain ranges unfold before me as I drove closer to Ashland. I realized my stomach had been aching with anticipation all day and it really ached as I drove past the sign that said, "Welcome to Ashland, Population 23,630".

I found my way to the ticket office and claimed my ticket. I found a little better parking spot trying to consider where would be a good place to sleep and not be bothered since if I waited until later the spots might start filling up as show time approached.

I then went sight seeing walking for a couple hours until I gauged it was time to go settle into a lawn spot at the outdoor amphitheatre. I had already eaten the dinner I had packed while visiting a nearby park so I just had my blanket to unfold and sit and wait for the performance.

I was about 30 minutes early so I read more of the play. The lawn started to fill. Close to show time a group noisily came and started setting up right beside me as few spots were left. They had lawn chairs and blanket, the largest cooler on wheels I had ever seen plus another smaller cooler. They started an elaborate set-up that included a vase with flowers, candle sticks, wine glasses and the good kind of paper plates that do not bend. The largest cooler had food and the smaller one wine. They were in good spirits and polite and asked me a couple times if they were in my viewing way. They settled in just before curtain, as I held my annotated *Hamlet* with theatre notes in my hands.

The words from the actors jumped out of their mouths and through the air like nothing one could read off a page. At times I would close my eyes and listen to the beauty of the language in the hands of the maestro Shakespeare.

During intermission a hunky boy from the group next to me noticed he was slightly sitting on a corner of my blanket. I was my own island. He noticed and smiled then extended a glass of wine to me and said, "may I pay my rent with a class of the Willamette Valley's finest chardonnay?"

I think he may have been in college and these were his fraternity and sorority friends. He had long hair like Bob Marley, I forget what they call that when you do not wash it and it grows long and braids naturally. He had on a tight fitting tie dye t-shirt, shorts and flip flops. I'll admit I was flattered and happy someone talked to me and could use a drink.

"Sure," I said.

He leaned over and handed me the glass, resting on his free elbow, then all in one motion moved over to sitting entirely on my blanket and grabbing the wine bottle with the hand he had just given me the glass.

"Since I moved to a bigger space here is my raised rent."

He set the bottle between us and the play resumed. His friends glanced over occasionally and one brought over an extra glass for him and said hello before heading back to the group. He did not speak during the play but occasionally looked over and smiled or raised his eyebrows during good scenes or dialogue. We drank the wine. It was a clear night and at times I looked up from the stage at the stars.

The play was nearing its end as Hamlet and Laertes were dueling and Prince Fortinbras was marching towards the castle. I wondered what I should say to this person next to me or what he would say to me.

Hamlet is dead.

"My friends and I are going over to Brug 9 would you like to join us? By the way I'm Axel."

"What's brat what?"

"Brug 9. It's a jazz club built under an old bridge."

"I probably shouldn't."

"Is it because I'm black?"

"Oh, no, I mean I'm Chinese and that did not stop you."

"So come on. Join our party. My friends and I are from Southern Oregon University. We're cool. I'm in grad school if that helps."

I began pulling up my blanket as Axel stepped off it, but had not said no. Axel helped me fold it then returned the empty wine bottle to the big cooler and appeared to be giving me space in case I did not want to go. His friends began walking towards the exit and he gave me a friendly, *come on you'll have fun,* look or it could have been a *come on and I'll attack you under this bridge that really has no nightclub* look. But, I followed Axel. I was trying to figure out the logistics when he said,

"We came in two VW vans, so you can ride in one of them and we'll bring you back here for I assume your car or if you want to follow us?"

"I'll follow you in my car."

"O.K. Come see where we're parked then we'll wait for you to get your car."

"Don't you need to ask them if they mind waiting and all?"

"One of the VWs is mine."

So I went to my car and gave up the choice parking spot and pulled up to the VWs and followed them to what in fact was a club built into and under a bridge.

Once inside, Axel asked me if he could get me a beer and I said I'll have a Carlsberg. He looked at me then said, "what's your second choice in case they don't have it?"

I said on impulse, "I'll have what you're having."

"O.K., but I'm a brandy and coke guy when I'm not seeing a play and drinking wine."

Axel went and came back with a Carlsberg.

"They had it and said they had a lot of European beers as they are based on a Dutch bar in Amsterdam that the owner went to once."

I took that as a sign and began to relax. We sat on wooden benches that ran along the tunnel shaped walls so that we were facing the other half of the patrons. The space in between was for dancing. The place was jammed so Axel was pressed up against me as we sat drinking and listening to the quartet on the make shift stage raised only six inches from the floor and with a red curtain behind it. Axel tapped his foot and tapped his free hand on his thigh. He had really well developed calf muscles. He smelled of sweat, but not in a bad way, just the way men smell. It was a humid night and we had been outside for about four hours. I hoped I smelled O.K. The band took a break. Axel turned to me with a big smile.

"I've given you wine and bought you a beer. Will you tell me your name or do I have to do dinner and a movie which is O.K. by me."

"Oh, my gosh, how rude, my name is Maggie. I guess I just forgot as it's been quite a night, my first time seeing *Hamlet* and now coming out with you and your friends."

"No problem."

"So Axel, what are you studying?"

"It's not so much what I'm studying. My thing is writing and so I take classes that will inspire or help my writing."

"That's neat. What do you write?"

"All kinds of stuff."

"Have you tried to get published? I have a friend at Future Tense Books, it's his small publishing company that he started while he works at Powell's Books."

"No. I don't want to be published."

"What? Why not?"

"Why does everyone think a writer wants to be published."

"I just thought …."

"I write to learn about what I think of myself and the world around me. Sometimes I can't get at my true feelings unless I process them through a fictitious character."

"But then don't you want to share that?"

"Why should I assume anyone else cares what I think? I'm not in it to become famous. Besides, with the Internet now, everyone knows everyone and what they think. How about you Maggie, what do you spend most of your time doing?"

"That's a great way to ask that. I'm a little sensitive now when people ask me what do I do since I just got laid off. I used to be an actuarial for Transamerica."

"Cool. So you could tell me what are the chances we might get together again? Like, what are the odds of us having ever met and now what will become of us?"

"Maybe not with the precision you might be thinking Axel."

"I'll get us a couple more beers before the band starts back and we can ponder that. I have a very precise idea Maggie."

I thought about what Axel said as he was getting the beers but could not make sense of it. When he returned he asked me, if I liked my old job.

"It kept me busy. That's what I miss. I am still learning how to keep myself busy."

"Why would you want to do that?"

"Fill the void, you know."

"No I do not. I choose not to try and distract myself with business or whatever you want to call it. Most people are very busy yet accomplish very little."

"You are a writer."

Axel laughed and clinked my beer bottle with his as if to say touché. What he said next just floored me on two levels.

"But really, the great philosopher Soren Kierkegaard warned of this because it's a tool people use to avoid difficult realities or maintain self-deceptions. Why do you think the Internet is so addictive?"

I am floored because he quoted a Danish philosopher to me on our first date, if that is what this is. He also quoted what is probably and I am only guessing because I know very little about Kierkegaard, the one thing that most resonates with me in this period of my life. I mean, I am a Chinese woman going Danish, how more distracting can you get to avoid reality?

Axel must have noticed my look, "hey sorry to have gotten all heavy and stuff. You're right I am such a writer, can't get out of my own head sometimes."

"No, you are fine, I am just an easy target right now to being sensitive. I wish I lived in Denmark?"

"Why?"

"It has the world's most generous unemployment benefits system, four years."

"Wow. That would be too tempting for me."

"I read that studies show that Danes are the happiest people on Earth, Axel."

"I'm not sure I would assume that is because the government takes care of them, Maggie. The money thing is all messed up right now. I read we owe China 1.4 trillion in debt, that's like $4500 per American. I don't think it helps our national security to owe one country so much, no offense."

"Maybe because we do they'll see to it that nothing happens to us."

"Whoa, that's a weird, but novel way to look at it. Allies in debt."

"Yeah, you know those young Chinese bankers are going to want their money."

"This is heavier than I wanted to go, can I just 360 here and say Maggie that you are beautiful. I hate to be cliché, but you are and so there. I love your almond shaped eyes. Is that racist or chauvinistic?"

"I don't think it's either. Keep talking."

"I love your pressed smile, like how it tightens your facial skin and makes it glow, like as if your cheeks had muscles. I love your long flowing dark brown but not black hair. It may be the light in here but it seems to be both colors at once. You have a delicate body and move your arms elegantly when you raise your drink to your mouth, your pinky hanging out alone under the bottle with nothing to hold onto. So forgive me. I've had a lot of classes in rhetoric, you know the art of persuasion, and so I know how to manipulate language and because of that I purposely don't. I don't lie and I don't try and shade the truth to convince someone of my position or to make someone think what I want them to think. I am saying you are beautiful because I think you are, no hidden agenda. It's just a fact as I see it. That's why I love to write, because when the truth is too raw even for me, I'll get one of my characters to say it."

I watched as the band made their way back to their instruments on the make-shift stage moving in slower than slow motion. I saw from the corner of my eye Axel's hand come across and rest on my knee. It was too aggressive a move to be taken as aggressive, if that makes any sense. I just did not feel threatened. I looked up at him without raising my head which must have made me look like an eighth grader asking, *what are you doing now?*

"Hey, before it gets loud in here again, let's cut out and go back to my place."

"What about your friends? Won't they need a ride home?"

"I'll let them know we're leaving. There's plenty of people we know here. They'll get by. We've done it before."

Axel said goodbye to his friends as I probably looked as sheepishly as I felt tearing him away from them. I wondered if they were thinking, *there goes Axel again, the Lady's Man,* or if they were thinking, *that's weird, he's never done that before,* or *she looks a little too old and too needy for him.*

It did not take us long to get to Axel's place, a house just off campus he shared with two roommates who he explained were both gone for the evening. Axel drove slow enough so as not to lose me in my car as I followed.

He showed me into the house and gave me a quick tour of the living room, kitchen and then into his room where he cleared a bean bag for me to sit in. He sat on his waterbed. We stared at each other for what seemed like a long time when he said he was going to go make some coffee. He then turned around after he went out the door and stuck his head back in the room and said, "Oh, you do like coffee?"

"Yes, thanks."

"Oh, and the bathroom is over there," he nodded his head sideways, then left again.

I managed to get myself out of the beanbag and went to the backroom. It was a typical single young guys bathroom, barely clean and with the toilet scrub brush near the toilet as a suggestion to anyone who might want to actually use it. I was hit hard by the feeling of the college campus scene, as if I had gone back in time, that my current journey required me to revisit the past before I could move beyond my current state and towards to my future.

Back in Axel's room, I waited alone and browsed his book self made with planks and cinder blocks. I looked at a section of books that contained the word he used at the club which I had heard before but had never really understood its meaning, rhetoric. He had several books on the subject, all by Wayne C. Booth entitled: *The Rhetoric of Fiction; A Rhetoric of Irony; Modern Dogma and the Rhetoric of Assent;* and *The Rhetoric of Rhetoric.* Plus two other titles by the same author, *The Company We Keep: An Ethics of Fiction;* and *Critical Understanding: The Powers and Limits of Pluralism.*

"See anything interesting?"

He was back with the coffee and found me sitting on the floor in front of the bookshelf. He sat down beside me setting the coffee cups between us.

"You have a lot of books by Booth."

"Yes, a professor at the University of Chicago. He died a few years ago."

"So what are your intentions Axel, no rhetoric, if that is the correct use of the term?"

"My intention is to sleep with you when you are ready and yes that will due for a proper contextual use of the term."

"I'm not ready, but I would like to stay until the morning and then head back if that is O.K.?"

"That is more than O.K. That is great."

We sipped our coffee. Axel put some music on his vintage turn table and we listened to jazz on an actual vinyl record.

"Do you have a spare T-shirt I could sleep in. I don't mean to be a bother."

"Sure. It's even clean."

Axel dug in his bureau top drawer and pulled out a T-shirt that he then put to his nose and smelled. He saw me looking at him and said, "just making sure." I went back into the bathroom and changed and was wearing the words "Make Japan Stop Dolphin Slaughter" on my chest.

Axel was already on the floor with a pillow and blanket.

"Oh, I did not mean for you to give up your bed."

"I am a gentleman as well as a good host. Have you ever slept on a waterbed?"

"No."

"You're in for a treat."

"I boarded the good ship Axel's waterbed and road the slight wave to the middle of the bed."

"It'll take a few minutes to get your bearings."

I lay in the middle letting myself be rocked and staring at a ceiling I could not see in the dark.

"I saw you have some Kierkegaard in your bookshelf."

"Yeah. I read once someone called him the Galileo of the inner world."

"I heard he was the father of existentialism."

"Yeah, this author explained that Kierkegaard was trying to tell us that we are more than just our minds and emotions. We can't let our mental or emotional flaws make us assume we cannot continue to strive for spiritual perfection. Isn't that great?"

I sensed Axel had sat up to make this point.

"To think Maggie that we do not have to believe that our true selves are completely anchored in our imperfect thoughts, feelings and actions, but that there is a part of us, sometimes trapped by our mental or emotional limitations that is still there saying to us, 'you can be better, just keep trying, your biology and environment may have set you back or may be getting in the way, but you don't have to give in to old patterns of assumption and negative mental constructs you maybe weren't even aware of forming.' I want to assume the best about a person until they show me otherwise, then I am just disappointed. I don't want to assume the worst in people and then be surprised that they are good and feel embarrassed for myself. Hey, Maggie, think about something tonight and sleep on it will you? I was planning on heading to Bend tomorrow to do some camping. You want to come with me?"

The nice thing about not having any specific place to be is that you can on fairly short notice find yourself looking at the Columbia Gorge along the Hood River. This morning Axel resolved my lack of clothes for a camping trip by loaning some more of his T-shirts to me and then making a quick stop at a Wal-Mart so I could get some undies and personals. My own mind had apparently either consciously or unconsciously already quickly decided it was safe to let this man I had just met the night before drive into a remote area of Oregon. Axel had loaded his VW van with a Coleman tent and stove, two sleeping bags and some food and water. We moved my car from its spot to his spot under his car port that the van had just vacated and we were off.

Bend

"It's really something to see here, Axel."

"Yeah, just a day's drive. To think if we had been on the Oregon trail in a covered wagon we could have only made about 15 miles a day, some of it maybe even had to be on foot. I remember looking at black and white photos of families on the trail during field trips as a kid to the Salem museum near the state capital. The faces of the parents and children in those photos looked so tired, who could blame them. I wondered, where are you going to end up and why are you going? Now I realize we are all wondering, heading west, if you will. We're meant to keep moving fueled by an interior journey."

"Is that what I'm doing here Axel?"

"That and your huge crush on me?"

I swung the tent bag I was holding and playfully hit Axel in his taut stomach. He smiled even broader and made like he was running away from me.

We "made camp" as Axel said, by pitching the tent, lining its floor with a plastic tarp then putting the sleeping bags in it.

We collected branches and twigs from the ground near the woods and Axel sawed a fallen limb he found deeper in the woods to make a few small logs.

We had a camp fire before dusk. Axel set up the Coleman stove and explained the camp fire would be for coffee and smores and that he would cook on the Coleman with some charcoal briquettes he had brought. He said tonight it was going to be beans and hamburgers, but tomorrow he would try to catch some fish for dinner.

The food was ready after the sun had set and we ate by camp fire light, the food tasting better than any other I had ever had.

"So Maggie do you speak Chinese," Axel asked while holding marshmallows over the fire on a hanger wire he had straightened out.

"I speak Cantonese which is spoken in Canton and Southern China, Hong Kong and Macau, as opposed to Mandarin which is the standard or official Chinese as spoken in Beijing, Northern and Southwestern China, most commonly spoken by most native speakers. I would love to go to China this year as the World's Fair is in Shanghai. The Expo there features a Danish pavilion designed by BIG, Bjarke Ingels's design firm. He got the Danish government to let him ship the Little Mermaid statue of the Hans Christian Anderson story from the Copenhagen harbor to the pavilion along with actual water from the harbor. It was all a very green endeavor as ships are often filled with water when returning empty to even their ballast."

Axel spread the now molten marshmallows on a graham cracker, added a Hersey's chocolate bar and another cracker and gave me the perfect smore. He then set about reloading his hangar with marshmallows for his smore.

"Do you speak any other languages, Axel?"

"No, but I am really interested in language, as you might guess, like the history of dictionaries and that sort of thing. Today while looking at the river, I thought of the first word in the Oxford English Dictionary, Second Edition, aa, pronounced "on" which means a stream or water course."

"That 's cool. What's the last word in the dictionary?"

"Zyrian. That's a member and the language of the Komi people of North Central Russia."

That night as we each lay in our sleeping bags and listened to the evening sounds of the woods and river, I thought of how much of my life I knew and was certain of just a few weeks ago and yet how little I knew then of what could lay around the bend when sent in a different direction. I had taught myself of an alternative Danish world and now was also part of Axel's very real world. I wish I could say I had quit my job to pursue this other me, what I sense is a truer me, but I was pushed out of the boat. For my part, I did take the initiative to learn about the Danish which led me to see *Hamlet* who introduced me to Axel.

> "Axel?"
> "Yes?"
> "You asleep?"
> "Obviously not."
> "I'm ready."

Terry

Axel drove me back to his place where I had left my car for our camping trip to Bend. Inside, he swapped a few things from his vehicle, clean clothes for the dirty ones and a few books instead of the camping gear, then he followed in his van behind me as I drove back to Portland.

As we drove I kept looking in my rear view mirror wondering how wise it was to have invited him for a few days stay and then how interesting it was that he accepted. He explained that being in graduate school, most of his classes were directed studies or directed reading where he just had to check in with his sponsoring professor once a month and could do the rest via e-mail. Plus, with winter semester about to start, he was at a good point for a change of scenery.

As our caravan of two approached Portland, the highway signage reminded me of my life here whereas I had been living what felt like a new life with Axel.

"Terry!" I shouted though no one was in my car. As we had passed under an overpass, I spotted Ms. Grandholm's terrier that I had been hired to find before my escape to see *Hamlet*. I am sure it was him rooting around under the bridge. I quickly pulled over and stopped at as safe a place on the shoulder of the highway as I could at the busy mix master that surrounds Portland and with it being rush hour the cars were really flying by me. I saw behind me Axel pull up and stop just inches before my rear fender. I watched him get out, careful to wait until cars went by so that they would not shear his door off. He came up to my window like a policeman and I rolled it down like a guilty speeder.

"Tough place to stop. Car trouble?"

"It's Terry."

"Who?"

"A dog I said I would help find. He's under the overpass. I have to try and get under there and rescue him."

"It's a little dangerous down there. I'll go. What am I looking for?"

"He's a black Terrier."

"Does he bite or hate black dudes?"

"I don't know."

I watched Axel work his way down the slope in his flip flops. I leaned over the railing and spotted Terry still there. I now could better see that what he was sniffing were the belongings of a homeless man sleeping in the corner of the overpass elbow. Terry was probably looking for food. Axel approached and when Terry saw him Axel stopped. Axel then took a granola bar out of his pocket, unwrapped it and put it on the ground just in front of him then backed up. Terry approached the granola bar, sniffed it and devoured it. Axel then took out another one and unwrapped it and when Terry was done with the first one, showed it to him but kept it in his hand. When Terry approached Axel picked him up and gave him the bar and then walked over and dropped a few dollars near the homeless man and then quickly came up the slope.

We still had some bottled water from our trip and we poured it in my Starbucks travel cup and let Terry slurp it with his tongue.

It was Terry all right, but the belly scratcher was right, no collar.

Ms. Grandholm was overjoyed at seeing Terry and he seemed to feel the same way. She thanked me and then thanked Axel.

Axel and I finally entered my apartment well after dark. I explained to him that we had just completed my first assignment as a private investigator. Axel said he wanted me to now call him Watson, since he had partnered with me to solve my first case.

We quickly got Axel settled in finding places for him to put his things while neither of us mentioned how long he might be staying. It did not take long for Axel to mention, "your place has a particular feel, like its all things Danish."

"Yes, I am very interested in the Danes and their culture and am going to visit Denmark, specifically Copenhagen someday."

"So is that why you went to see *Hamlet*?"

"Yes."

"So I can thank Shakespeare for meeting you."

"You say very nice things sometimes, Axel."

What with the play, camping trip, drive back and rescuing Terry, we had neglected to plan anything for New Years and now the evening was upon us and we realized it was almost midnight. I found some apple juice in the refrigerator and once Axel was done putting the last of his few things up and taking a quick shower from the drive up, I handed him a glass and we toasted the new year.

This year really feels new to me.

Axe

I could not help but smile while making coffee this morning. It is a beautiful new year's, clear, bright and crisp, not cold. Plus, Axel is here, along with his grooming products now placed in my bathroom called Axe which I find endlessly amusing. Axe shampoo and conditioner in one. Axe deodorant and anti-perspirent. Axe hair jell and moose. The hair care products surprised me because I did not think he washed his hair the way he wore it, but maybe he was thinking of making a change. Is it not comically ironic that his name is Axel and the products are Axe?

"What are you smiling about," Axel asked me as he came into the kitchen and I handed him a mug of coffee.

"Axe me later," I said, and giggled.

"What?"

"Never mind."

"O.K., so Maggie what do you want to do today, first day of the new year and all?"

We sat down with our mugs at the kitchen table. I had set in the middle of the table milk, brown sugar, honey, cinnamon and nutmeg in case Axel wanted to add anything to his coffee. He did not.

Axel was already dressed in what I have come to think of as his Axel uniform because I have yet to see him wear anything else. His uniform is made up of flip flops, shorts and a t-shirt with some kind of insignia. Today it reads, "this is the oldest I have been so far."

"I need to start on my next case. Watching on television last night the year change across the globe with all the fireworks, especially in China, reminded me of my next assignment."

I explained to Axel that since my unemployment, I could now talk about my layoff as if it was something that happened to someone else, I had been given $100 as a retainer by Mr. Woo to find his missing nephew Dang.

"But, Axel, you can take it easy and relax today. I know a lot of people watch bowl games of college football."

"No, I'm not much of a T.V. watcher. I'll help you Maggie with your work. Remember, I'm your Watson."

"O.K."

"O.K., great. Where do we start? I know, Maggie you tell me what you know so far and we'll go from there."

"Well, Dang was supposed to visit Portland. His family put him on a plane in China, but he never arrived when Mr. Woo's family went to pick him up in Portland."

"That's it?"

"That's all I know at the moment."

"I see. This reminds me of Edgar Allen Poe's, short story, *the Purloined Letter*, in that the main character and his partner try to figure out a mystery of where an important letter has been hidden. Despite the apartment in question where the letter is known to have been hidden being searched top to bottom by the authorities, the letter is still unaccounted for. Without ever going to the apartment, while sitting and discussing the matter with each other, through careful deduction, logic and mathematical analysis, they arrive at the conclusion that the letter is hidden in the letter holder on the desk. That's why it has yet to be found. It is the only place that must not have been searched since a letter holder is so absurdly obvious a place to hide a letter."

"How does this relate to that?"

"Well, you have a missing person rather than a letter, but I think your solution is potentially as obvious. If we can confirm that he really did get on the flight, then the only solution is that he got off it before Portland. To confirm he got on the flight, since you won't be given access to airline records, you'll need to find out if someone saw him go through the jet bridge and waited while they pulled it away from the plane to confirm he did not come back out. If that is confirmed then we know we don't have to start looking for him in China. We have to then check if the plane made any stops before Portland. That should be easy enough. An airline would tell you that on a past flight, I'm guessing. Otherwise, you'd think his family knew if his ticket was direct or not. I'm guessing due to the distance it is very unlikely he had a direct flight."

"O.K., sounds like I have a few calls to make today."

"Yep, hopefully you can reach his family and the airlines are 24/7/365, so calling them on New Year's should be no problem."

"I know China is 15 hours ahead of us, so if it is 10 in the morning now here it is 1 a.m. there. So I better wait about seven hours to call Dang's folks."

"In the meantime, can you call Mr. Woo and at least find out what airline they went to pick him up at so you can call them and see if they have direct flights?

"He gave me Dang's family's number in China but I did not think to ask for his and I know he is closed today for the holiday."

"Looks like we are cooling our jets until tonight, Maggie, no pun intended."

"Yeah, I did not prepare very well for this. I don't even have Dang's full name yet."

"Are you sure this is what you want to do Maggie? Find people? It does have an element of potential danger. What if he does not want to be found?"

"I never thought of that. Axel, why are you so good at this. Way better thn me. You just think it through more."

"It's my apophenia, probably."

"Your what?"

"Apophenia, it's kinda a phobia although I don't think it's recognized yet by the handbook of psychiatry. Recognized disorders have to make it into that book to be accepted by the psychiatric community is my understanding."

"Yes, but back to apophinia, Axel, if I said it right."

"It's where you see pattern and combinations in otherwise random things. Ever since I can remember, I found meaning in what others could only see as meaningless and unrelated. Where others looked at facts or events as unconnected, I seemed to find connections."

"Sounds like a great phobia to have."

"Another thing I thought of Maggie, is to ask his family if he has a cell phone, e-mail or if he is on Facebook. These might be a ways to potentially communicate with him."

"Great. I never thought of just maybe trying to reach out to him."

"It's weird, some people may not answer a call from their family, but might from a stranger out of curiosity. Again, as a friend, I want to warn you of the potential danger. People that disappear are often not victims but are into something maybe not so good. We're not powerful people Maggie, we're not Zuckerberg or the Google guys. We're not billionaires with tons of resources and assets like they call them in the Bourne movies."

"Well, we got two good brains. That's the American Way, right? We have our own human capital and desire. Our advantage is that we have no advantage. Therefore, we can operate under the radar."

Caroline Wozniacki

Axel and I spent the rest of New Year's day lounging around. He read and I played on my computer. I found I could watch a tennis match from Copenhagen. It was a women's tennis event called the Copenhagen Open Classic, sponsored by Carlsberg and I learned that the Danish player I was watching, Caroline Wozniacki was not only Denmark's best player but was ranked number one in the world. The commentators spoke excellent English and mentioned during a break in the action that Denmark had lost a famous sports figure over the weekend, Bent Larsen, a former Chess Grandmaster. I had never really thought of chess as a sport, but I could see how others did as they described his successes in the seventies against the Soviets. A moment of silence they said would be observed next week at the Politiken Cup, Denmark's annual international chess tournament.

Axel came over to see what I was doing with a finger between his book where he had left off reading and seemed annoyed to discover what I was watching. I sensed that besides not being too into sports he did not think much of surfing the internet, despite seemingly to know a lot about it.

What was not to like about the internet? I had just learned about Bent Larsen and Caroline Wozniacki.

That night I called the number that Mr. Woo's daughter had given me for Dang's parents, but no one answered. I looked at my phone display screen and confirmed I had dialed the right numbers. I tried it again with operator assistance, but with the same result. No answering machine engaged, after the eight rings I allowed each time.

Maybe they were away for the holidays or maybe sleeping in from too much New Year's celebrating.

January 2, 2011

Although it is Sunday, I take a chance that Mr. Woo might be open after New Year's day. Since I did not get through to Dang's parents, I am hoping he or his daughter remembers what airline they tried to pick him up at so that I can make some calls while waiting to get through to Dang's parents. I had never dropped off my cleaning on a Sunday, always Saturday or during the week and had never noticed if his sign had said anything about Sunday hours. It is a mild sunny day so my bike ride is very pleasant. I left Axel at the kitchen table where he was proof reading a paper he had to turn in next week.

Woo's Dry Cleaning is closed. The sign confirms it, too. I did not know where he lived. So I ride home.

I am a little down on myself, as not getting through to Dang's parents and not being able to talk to Mr. Woo remind me I left for *Hamlet* when I could have started my investigation. Maybe Dang has already turned up?

Once home, I made some notes on what to ask Dang's family should I make contact and practiced the translation into simple Chinese so that I would be better prepared than what I had been so far. I wrote in a notebook:

> What airline did Dang fly and what day and city did he leave from?

航空公司没有什么党，什么飞一天，他离开城市的？

> Does he have a phone with him?

他有他的电话？

> What is his full name?

他的全名是什么？

I try Dang's parents again tonight, but with the same results. Then Axel and I make dinner.

Monday

Mr. Woo, once he understood what I was asking, did not know the answer to any of my questions and could not remember what airline his daughter had driven him to pick up Dang at the Portland airport. His daughter was not working this Monday and I took him to mean when he said three times in succession, "no work Monday" that she normally had Monday off.

As I rode my bike back to my apartment I thought the trip was not a waist as I did learn that Dang must still be missing as Mr. Woo did not mention he had heard from him or that I should stop looking.

I try Dang's family again tonight. No luck.

Tuesday

I dropped Axel off at Kate's Yoga and Espresso so that he would not get cabin fever and could work out while visiting. I had offered to drive us, but Axel said he would jog along my bike as I rode. I introduce him to Kate and withstand her furtive glances at me and all those questions that just go to the edge of *are you getting married* or words to that effect. Axel gave me a kiss goodbye to heighten the drama which I took as his sense of humor since he had never kissed me before when we were separating for the day. Kate took it in knowingly. As he headed into the next yoga class, I headed off to Woo's Cleaners.

Mr. Woo's daughter said they went to the China Southern Airlines terminal to meet Dang on November 22. I told her I was impressed she recalled the date. She said she remembers it because she was watching a story on the Kennedy assassination on the outside terminal monitor.

I had my first lead, a place to finally start.

Before I left I asked her a few more questions I should have earlier. Dang's full name is Dang Chou Ming. His parents do have an e-mail address and can also be texted as the number I was given is to a cell phone, but Mr. Woo's daughter could not recall if it was the Mom's or the Dad's. I found out Mr. Woo's daughter's first name is Mindy.

I also asked Mindy a favor, if she would please call or e-mail Dang's parents and let them know who I was and what her father had asked me to do, by way of introduction.

Mindy, put down the pile of men's shirts she had just collected in her arms and gave me the impression that I just asked for one thing too many, I had broken the last straw of her patience. Although she did not say anything more then "O.K." before she picked up the shirts again just as suddenly as she had set them down while heading into the back room, the impression I came away with was that she did not think much of her father enlisting me.

Riding away I imagined Mindy as studying molecular biology while working at her father's business to help pay tuition and help her family. I imagined her as the smart overachieving Asian woman I used to think I was.

Wednesday

China Southern Airways had no problem telling me about their past flights as that raised no security breaches. They would not give out any passenger names but did confirm that on November 22 of last year they had a U.S. bound flight that left Guangzhou which is the only city they fly out of in Canton province. It first made a stop in Shanghai to pick up more passengers before flying on to Copenhagen where it left for JFK/Portland two days later.

I asked the representatives on the phone why the flight would not head east and cross the Pacific. She responded that most of their U.S. bound flights do in fact land first in Los Angeles before going on to Portland and then Seattle and back to Canton, but some head for Europe depending on bookings. She explained that some like a couple days in Europe along the way. Makes for a nice vacation, she added, especially for young students.

My lead had blossomed into several possible scenarios. As Axel and I discussed them that night over wine we realized Dang could have not boarded the flight originally or could have gotten off and not gotten back on in Shanghai, Copenhagen or New York.

That night, in my best Cantonese, I e-mailed Dang's family using the e-mail address Mindy had given me. I introduced myself, said Mindy would also confirm my reason for contacting them, asked the question I had earlier prepared about whether he had a phone with him and then added a further question on if it had e-mail capability.

Thursday

Tonight I received a response from China. The e-mail was in English, so I guessed they had used Google translation and it said the following:

> We are grateful you are joining the search for Dang. He does have a cell phone and e-mail access. He has not answered our calls. His e-mail is DangNabIt@gmail.com. He loves American slang. Dung Chao Ming.

I toss and turn as Axel snores. I am wondering what my next move should be tomorrow. If I e-mail Dang and he does not want to be found then he will not respond or become suspicious and harder to find. If he cannot answer his phone because he has lost it or is hurt or dead than calling or e-mailing is useless.

Friday

"Facebook," I asked as Axel devoured an egg sandwich I just watched him meticulously make, the yoke dripping down his fingers.

"Yes, I think Facebook is the answer to the dilemma you are facing," he said between mouthfuls.

I had shared with Axel my quandary that had kept me up most of the night.

"You see Maggie, if he does not want to be found then he needs to be approached as if you are not looking for him. So, if we search Facebook for his name and get lucky enough to find it, then you request to be his friend. He'll then just think of you as another friend of a friend wanting to be his friend. We'll have taken a nice picture of you to entice him, I am going to assume he is not gay or we can later try a picture of me and if he accepts we'll be into his world and maybe gain some clues as to where he is at."

"I did not think China had Facebook. They barely have Google."

" True, but many of them can hack into it or go through European web routers. Let's not assume until we try."

So we checked that my Facebook account was still up and running and then Axel went through my closet and came out with a v-neck knit top. I put it on and it was a bit small and tight on me.

"Perfect," he said.

"I thought this was going to be a nice picture, you said."

"Nice and enticing."

Axel moved my coffee table to the center of the living room. I located my camera and made sure it came on and did not have dead batteries.

"O.K., kneel and then lean on the coffee table with your elbows."

"Oh, come on," I protested. My cleavage was almost completely pressed together as I did this. "Is this for him or you?"

"I might keep a copy if it turns out good."

Axel backed up and centered my digital camera and took some shots, as I do my best to press on the table with my elbows and simultaneously press my arms into my sides and make myself seem more busty. I know the shot he is after. He stops to view the ones he has taken.

"Great. I got several that will work."
He set the camera down and moved quickly toward me.

Saturday

Axel looked awkward as he came into the kitchen this morning to get his coffee.

"Maggie, uh, sorry I went caveman on you last night, but the pict...."

"You didn't hear me complaining. I could go for round two tonight."

"Great, but I'm taking a nap this afternoon, to get ready. I'm wiped out."

"I downloaded one of the pictures and updated my Facebook account with it. I just came to grab some coffee, too and am about to search for Dang on Facebook."

We set our mugs on the kitchen table near my laptop and I began my search for Dang Chou Ming. I typed his name into the "search for your friends" site on Facebook and to my surprise, three such names came up. Two of the three had pictures and the other one had a Slim Pickins picture, the old Hollywood actor, comedian. Axel, looking over my shoulder says, "well, the good news is his name comes up. Bad news is you now have to try and get a picture of him from Woo or the family. They can probably scan you one."

"I think it's him," I said pointing to Slim.

"Maggie that's some old actor, I can't remember his name, but whoever posted that as his Facebook thumb is probably 75 years old."

"Axel, it's something in the e-mail, his e-mail is DangNabIt and his father said he has quite a love for American slang. In the movie Dr. Strangelove, Slim Pickins plays a cowboy hat wearing fighter pilot who always says, "dang nab it.""

"Wow, that's good detective work. Let's give it a try."

I sent a message to the Dang with the Slim Pickins photo requesting friending. Axel and I then waited.

We turned on the television and watched President Obama host the Chinese President Hu Jintao at the White House where they were holding a joint press conference. President Jintao looked nothing like former Chinese leaders in their army green pajama like clothes in honor of Mao. He wore a business suit with crisp white shirt and blue silk tie. He looked like the CEO of Toyota. I got up off the couch periodically, negotiating over Axel's thighs and legs to check my e-mail, but no acceptance yet from the Dang Slim Pickins.

Sunday

No word from Dang/Slim last night, so I am checking my Facebook account this morning.

"Axel, can you get in here please."

Axel came into the kitchen which is now our joint office still wiping his body with a towel from his shower.

"Look, I've been accepted as a friend by Dang Slim."

"Great. Go onto his home page and let's see what he's about."

Dang/Slim has 743 friends. There are the usual pictures of people and places. I scroll down to view past postings. Maybe it was because my eyes were trained to spot Denmark references, but I noticed the word Copenhagen in one post and slowed down my scrolling to read,

"Hey, Red, see you soon. What Kippe in Copenhagen should we meet at?"

It was a post from Dang/Slim as it had Slim's picture by it.

"Axel, Dang's flight was to stop in Copenhagen."

"Really?"

"Yeah. I wonder who Red is?"

"I wonder what Kippe means?"

I scrolled down some more.

"Stop," Axel said.

"What?"

"There, look. Look at the redhead."

I look at the picture Axel is pointing to of a cute young woman with short cropped red hair that is somewhat spiked. Her back is to the camera and she is turning around towards it so one sees only three quarters of her face which is smiling and appears to be saying, "look at my butt, it's cute." Her name appears as Bridgit.

"You think that is Red, Axel?"

"Yes, I think he is meeting a girl. Look up Kippe on Google ."

Kippe, Danish, bar or inexpensive tavern, café.

We both said simultaneously,

"He's meeting Bridget at a bar in Copenhagen."

"The post is pretty recent so let's keep monitoring Slim's Facebook page and see if she gives him a Kippe to go to," Axel said.

"Then what? What do we do when we learn where they are going to meet? So what? What do I do then Axel?"

"That is a good question for which I do not have an answer. Let's just wait and see what comes up. It may then give us an idea."

We spent the afternoon periodically checking Slim's Facebook page and working on Axel's latest paper that he was writing for school. The topic was on the growing science of Nano technology. Axel was using it as a metaphor for a literary theme he was developing that I do not quite understand and so cannot explain. I acted as his proof reader to try and catch typos that spell check might miss. I often read over his shoulder to save paper rather than print out and in this way he could make corrections on the spot as I pointed them out. It also gave me a chance to periodically rub his chest and mess with him.

Monday

That morning there were two posts on Slim's Facebook.

Maggie, what up in Portland? Dang.

Dang, meet me at the Marriott's bar. Red.

Over breakfast I briefed Axel as my laptop sat contently with its loaded inbox between us on the kitchen table as if waiting for our decision on what to do next.

"So he now knows me and where I live," I said.

"Power of the internet. I guess it's only fair since we want to know about him," Axel said.

"I probably should have used a fake name and profile. What if he's up to no good?"

Axel did not respond, which I took to mean he felt guilty about not thinking of that himself and instead getting all horny after taking my picture. I should have thought of it, but it seemed like such a shot in the dark. I do not think I was expecting any response or that there was even the remote possibility of it being Dang. I was used to not responding to unsolicited friend requests but have never initiated one of my own.

"I didn't know Marriott was in Copenhagen? Doesn't sound like a cheap bar to me. Guess Red has expensive tastes," Axel finally said.

"I have to think this through, Axel. He wants to communicate with me and he wants to meet Red or Bridgit at the Marriott bar."

That night I tossed and turned again as I slept on my options. Should I let Dang's family know now that I might have found him, although I could not be completely sure? Should I let the authorities know and let them pursue the lead? Should I call or e-mail Dang and simply ask him, are you the Dang hiding from your family?

All Things Danish, Frank G. Merlino, Copyright 2011

Tuesday

Axel and I discussed the pros and cons of the options I had come up with overnight as we ate breakfast.

"If Dang has good reason to be hiding", Axel began, wiping egg yoke from his lips with his napkin, "then letting his parents know or the authorities may not be so good and he certainly would not tell you if you asked."

"So where does that leave me, should I give Mr. Woo his money back and say I am over my head?"

"Well, only if you really feel that way."

"And if I want to see this through?"

"Then you might have to, as they say in the military, 'develop the situation.'"

"Axel, what is that and what do you know about the military?"

"It means developing more facts by talking to people on the ground or on site. I read a lot, remember."

"Right. So how do I get more facts and talk to these ground people?"

"It is most effective done face to face."

75

"Sounds potentially dangerous."
"That's why it's a military thing. They are specially trained."

Sunday

My stomach began to jump, not because I do not like flying but because Copenhagen was unfolding below me as dawn broke and our plane was preparing to land after our flight across the Atlantic. Axel is still asleep, his head leaning to my side, snoring and a bit of drool dotting the side of his lip.

It had been a hectic two and a half weeks as we shopped for the best air fare, Axel went back to his place to get a few extra things and let his roommates know he was going to Denmark for a month and I let Mr. Woo and Dang's family know I had a lead and would get back to them.

I had decided to "develop the situation" and go meet Dang in Copenhagen. I had sent him a message saying I was an art student and was coming to study and would like to meet him at the Marriott since I thought he liked it since he mentioned it on his page. He had responded in the affirmative. We were meeting tomorrow.

Axel and I were using our savings. I explained to him my Danish thing and that I had always wanted to go to Copenhagen anyway. He decided he would come rather than let me go alone and suggested I write it off as a business expense on my taxes since I was technically working.

I was amazed how easy it was to up and live my dream and come to Copenhagen. Although, I cried the night before we left. Axel had returned with his extra things and we were both packed and went to sleep early. As we lay in bed I began to cry because of how few people I needed to tell where I was going. Axel comforted me by saying he had just told his roommates since he was estranged from his family and then said, "we have each other."

Copenhagen

It is very cold as Axel and I step out of the airport terminal and into Danish air. Why would it not be as it is February and I am as close to the arctic circle as I have ever been. This is my first time overseas. I am not counting weekend trips to the Caribbean with girlfriends. My research told me this was a dark season for Denmark and the Danish are often quite moody until spring and the additional hours of light.

I love it all so far. Hearing the language and seeing the cherub like beautiful blond faces of the people. I keep thinking of reindeer, but am not sure why. Maybe it is because of all the wool hats with tie strings dangling down the sides and furry balls at the ends. I make a mental note to buy one, but right now we hurry as the meeting with Dang is tomorrow. There will be time for sight seeing and souvenirs later.

We find a cab and ask to be taken to The Hamlet. Yes, I found a very moderately priced hotel near the Marriott where we will meet Dang called Hamlet. I booked it regardless of whether it turns out to be a dump, the karma is too much to pass up.

We strain our necks and take in the city around us from the window of the cab, turning our heads all around us as we are driven. I love everything I see.

The cab pulls up to The Hamlet. Its exterior has a chalet like look with black and brown painted wood trim and window boxes where summer flowers might later bloom. We pay the cab driver with the Krones we had exchanged at the airport for our dollars.

Inside it is all beige, grey and gold with the smell of citrus grass. I may never leave this place. The receptionist is very polite and speaks perfect English. She does not seem at all moody or depressed by the gray day or early darkness that will arrive at mid
day.

The room, well, it is crisp. Crisp is the key word so far. The place looks crisp. The people are crisp. Copenhagen is crisp.

Axel let me shower first. I spent the first ten minutes in the bathroom putting the complimentary toiletries in and out of my travel bag. First thinking I would save them for when I would be back in Portland to remind me of the trip, then deciding to use them now and enjoy all the scents and fragrances of this new place. I finally decided to use them and enjoyed a luxuriant bath with sea salts and seaweed body wash.

After his shower Axel ordered us room service and we enjoyed a late lunch early dinner. Axel studied up on Danish cuisine before we left. We had cod cakes, salads with herring and gooseberry tarts. We also had Aquavit, my contribution suggestion to the meal selection. It was strong and went well chased down by some bottled water. Axel tried the Aquavit, but said he would stick to coffee as his drug of choice.

After the meal we climbed into bed and explored Danish television. We lingered at the international CNN station because it was familiar. Before we knew it we had fallen asleep.

I woke up with a fright thinking it was tomorrow and we had missed our meeting with Dang. Once my mind truly awakened and I recalibrated where I was and confirmed the time, I realized it was only midnight Copenhagen time. I called the front desk as quietly as I could as Axel was still asleep and asked for a six a.m. wake-up call. I then also set my travel alarm as a back-up.

Before climbing back in bed next to Axel, I looked out the room window to Copenhagen below at night. I thought to myself, *I am really here.* I could not help feel some pride. I had dreamed of coming to Denmark and now I was here working on a job I had developed for myself.

Back in bed, nestling against Axel, I felt glad to be taking a chance on love. I could not have imagined a few months ago at the nadir of my self-image that I would be in Copenhagen with him to start the new year. As his belly raises up and down to the rhythm of his breathing, my hand resting on it, I wonder what he is dreaming of or what his subconscious is thinking of right now. Is it, wow this is great to be here with the love of my life? Or is it, wow they have great food here? Or, I can write about this experience. Or is his deeper subconscious remembering an old girlfriend and he is dreaming of being back with her or wondering if he should have stayed with her?

Copenhagen – Day Two

The phone ring jolts me upright with its clanging repetition. I answer to hear the pre-recorded voice greet me good morning and announce it is six o'clock. My travel alarm goes off as I am hanging up which elicits a moan from Axel before I turn it off.

I feel like a new person getting out of bed as Axel turns over fighting the start of the day. I throw the curtains open to welcome the Copenhagen morning which gets Axel finally moving. I let him shower first and look at the newspaper that I heard placed outside our door.

After we dress, breakfast and a quick cab ride we enter the Marriott lobby. I take some of the brochures on Copenhagen and the surrounding communities as we make our way to the one of the thin cushioned sectionals to sit and wait for someone who we do not know what he looks like, but who knows what I look like. While waiting I think of all the things I should have done beforehand like have a picture of Dang scanned to me by his parents or ask Dang what he would be wearing or get his cell phone number or give him mine. I continue

to feel inadequate as a detective. We wait
and wait. I read all the brochures.

"I think we should ask the front desk
if there is a message or something, because I
think he is going to be a no show," Axel
finally offered from over his laptop lid while
still typing.

I get up and go over to a tall, thin
attendant with blond hair and gold wire
rimmed glasses. He acknowledges me
before I even get there.

"Yes, good morning."

"Good morning. I am waiting for a
friend but he is very late. I am wondering if
he might have left a message. Is there a
message from Dang Choa Ming?"

"Mr. Ming checked out earlier
today."

I never considered he might be
staying here. Duh. What is wrong with me?
Something made me ask, "What room was
he in?"

The attendant raised an eyebrow
over his gold rim. I think he was
considering what harm was there to tell the
room number of someone who is not there
anymore. I smiled as warmly as I could.

"1425," he said.

I smiled and nodded and headed
back to Axel. I give him a quick update and

announced we are going up to 1425.

"Why are we going to a room no one is in?"

"Clues."

"What if the maids have been through already?"

"What if they haven't been?"

We exit the elevator on the fourteenth floor and navigate around the maid carts in the hallway. We find 1425. There is a cart next to it and a maid cleaning the next door room. The door to 1425 is closed.

"Excuse me," I say to the maid in the room next door. Speak English?"

"Yes."

"Excuse me for interrupting, but I need in to 1425 before I leave the hotel."

She quickly put down the sheets she had pulled and let me in to 1425 so as to get back to her work.

"Maggie, are we breaking and entering," Axel asked.

"Well, we did not break anything and we are simply in a room that no one is in. I did not lie. She just assumed we had just checked out and turned our keys in and remembered we had forgotten something. She probably figured she was too busy to call the Manager who she probably can't often get right away and with your laptop bag you and I look like we might have just stayed here."

"O.K., Sherlock, good work I will grant you that. I think we should hurry though."

"Right, Watson."

Axel and I looked through the room. I looked in the bedroom and Axel in the bathroom. It was fairly clean except for the rumbled just slept in bed. Since hotel rooms are cleaned each day, it is hard to determine how many nights he stayed here. I looked in the waste basket and pulled out a small, shiny, crumpled piece of paper. It was a boarding pass from a flight last week on Air Luxembourg to Copenhagen. What was he doing in Luxemburg?

"I got something," Axel said from the bathroom.

Axel showed me a scrap of notepad paper with what seemed like a phone number scribbled on it in felt tip pen.

"I found it in the waste basket near a disposal razor, soap wrappers, dental floss and Kleenex. It was a little gross pulling it out. You are welcome."

"Thank you. I found this old boarding pass in the other waste basket."

We did one more pass of the room, Axel looking under the bed while I told him it was probably boarded like most hotels, but he came up from under it with a torn out magazine article.

"I wonder if this was his or if the cleaning staff missed it and it was someone else's?"

Axel said leafing through, "looks like an article on clean energy."

We looked at each other and agreed it was time to go.

Grundtvig Church

I feel dwarfed as Axel and I sit outside the giant Grundtvig Church in the Bispebjerg District of Copenhagen. The church looms over us in the outdoor café set up for tourists to have coffee after touring the inside or in our case before our tour. I had seen a picture of the church in one of the brochures I picked up at the Marriott and we have come here to review the evidence we collected and talk about our next course of action. The church's three stepped gables with vertical brick-beading cast shadows across Axel's face as he sits across me sipping his coffee. It's sharp geometries making patterns on the ground. Some tables have umbrellas, but they are all closed as the rare sunlight seems welcome by the patrons. A child unsteadily rides what appears to be a new bicycle across the square as her mother walks closely behind and occasionally reaches out her hand to touch the seat and steady the ride.

"It says the church was designed by P.V. Jensen-Klint," I say reading the brochure, "in 1922".

"I think we should call that telephone number we found and see what it is," Axel said.

I dial the number and get the Marriott we were just at.

"The number was written on a scrap of paper that has the words, 'Frog's Tooth', maybe that's a bar or a restaurant, see if information can give you a number. Maybe Dang wrote the number of the Marriott while there or someone who had been there wrote it for him."

So I called information next and they had no listing of a Frog Tooth in Copenhagen.

"No luck. No listing by that name."

"So what we got so far is that he was in Luxembourg. He may have been reading about clean energy and our last clue is something Frog Tooth," Axel summarized.

We sat silently looking at the boarding pass, article and phone number.

"Let's take the tour," I finally said.

"One more second," Axel said still staring at the evidence, "I am trying to see if my synethesia can help."

"Your what?"

"Synesthesia is a condition where you see numbers as colors. Each number 0 to 9 has its own color. I am looking at the flight number, phone number and any numbers in the article to see if I can detect a pattern. Remember I told you I also had apophania, seeing patterns where none would be expected."

"And? Anything?"

"Not yet…I was also focusing on the gate number and time of boarding and departure. Maybe after the tour something will hit me. By the way, did you know today is Chinese New Year's. February 3. Yep, year of the Rabbit. Happy New Year, again, well based on the Chinese zodiac calendar anyway."

"Always something interesting with you, Axel."

"Thanks. You're pretty out there yourself."

Canal Tour

After the church tour, Axel and I find ourselves floating on the canals of Copenhagen. He has his arm around me and we sit and enjoy the sights in the open air boat. I marvel at the pastel colored building on either side. Bicyclists speed across overhead as we pass under bridges. I am reminded that Copenhagen is thought to be the most eco-minded of cities which then reminds me of the article we found in Dang's room. Is that why he is here? Is he an engineer for an energy company that maybe makes solar panels?

As we go along I realize that Copenhagen is actually closer to Sweden than its own mainland Denmark. Our boat passes the spot where the Little Mermaid sculpture honoring the Hans Christian Anderson story is normally, except it is an empty pedestal now as the tour guide explains what I had learned already that it was shipped to Shanghai for the World's Fair exhibit for Denmark.

"So do you believe in God?" Axel's question startles me out of my own thoughts. "I ask because the church tour got me thinking Maggie. All that beauty. Is it just architecture or is there something spiritual going on? I am sure the designer thought there was something spiritual in what he was doing, maybe even imagining he was being like The Great Designer. I don't think you take a church as a commission and not have some spirituality in you. I can't believe it would be seen as just a payday by the architect, but who knows, right? I think I believe in a Great Designer, but not one that attends to our every detail. I think that's where natural selection takes over. I believe in The Spark."

Axel turned to me and starred. I think he was thinking, *now it's your turn.*

"I was raised Buddhist. I know that is not really a religion as it is more a way of approaching life. I guess I would say that I don't disbelieve in a higher being, I just can't say I believe. But I'm open."

"I just think there is too much pattern in the world for this all to be random and heading for a chaotic end where nature just consumes us eventually by our own destruction or eco-system calamity," he added and then turned away and starred out into the canal.

Jazzhus Montmartre Club

"I think that this was a pretty full day. Cheers." Alex and I toasted with our Carlsbergs and listened to the jazz trio in front of us. The Jazzhus Montmartre Club had been closed for years according to BluePlanet having once been called the "high temple" of the European jazz scene drawing even Miles Davis for extended weeks. It reopened this year with the promotion of "come to the rebirth of cool". I thought Axel would like it and he does. He said he saw himself as a goateed, beret wearing guy.

"Why so glum, Maggie," Axel asked.

"Oh, I just was thinking, what if we get no more clues and this all comes to a dead end?"

"Two things. One, if it does, then we are having and will continue to have a great time seeing this great city. Two, let's do an internet search on Luxembourg and see what's going on there and why Dang might have been there."

That did brighten my mood and I buried myself into my PDA and Axel took out his laptop and we set to work, ordering another round of beers, as well.

"Wow. It's only 998 square miles," I said.

"Yeah, called the Grand Duchy of Luxembourg to be precise," Axel contributed.

"It's surrounded by Belgium, France and Germany," I countered as if in a tennis match.

"Oh, hold the phone."

"What," I asked looking up at Axel.

"Luxembourg just hosted a world wide conference on clean energy called the World Green Forum."

"Do you think Dang was there for that, based on the article we found under the bed? Axel, I think he is a corporate spy trying to steal some company's energy cell technology or hybrid vehicle secrets."

I excused myself to go to the bathroom saying, "too much beer be right back" leaving Axel still chuckling over my Dang grassy knoll theory and still searching on his laptop.

Once at the mirror washing my hands I noticed the woman next to me putting on her lipstick. I was admiring her skinny jeans when I saw it. Her t-shirt. It said, "Frog Tooth". She was putting her

lipstick in her purse and so I had to ask
quickly.

"Excuse me. What does your t-shirt
mean?"

She turned and looked at me with a
friendly face and said in a clipped English
that sounded more German than Danish,

"It is club in Norrebro."

"Norr...?"

"Norrebro. It is working class
district much near here."

"Thanks. Thank you."

I rushed out and went back to Axel
still sipping his beer legs crossed, foot
tapping in mid air.

"We've got to go to Norrebro. It's
not far. It's wear Frog Tooth is. I'll explain
as we go. Drink up and I'll pay our bill."

"O.K. I got the tip."

Axel chugged his beer and we were
out on the street. We hurry along passing
other evening couples enjoying bar hopping.
I stop some of them to direct us and we
eventually turn a corner and see a neon sign
with the words Frog Tooth spelled out in
individual block panels of different colors.
Very art deco and probably giving Axel fits,
then I remembered it was numbers he saw in
colors that were not there not letters that are
in color.

Inside we are greeted by a giant stuffed frog with one large buck tooth. It is near the podium where hostesses wearing the shirt I saw in the bathroom are taking names to be seated. I see beyond them to a large room lined with shelves of books and paintings. The patrons all seem clad in black. I imagined that during the day some worked for government agencies sorting microfilm and the others were graduate students. A DJ was in the corner playing world techno dance type music.

"Would you like the dessert side or the appetizer side of the room," we were asked by the hostess once we came to our turn at the podium.

Axel and I looked at each other and then he said, "any chance we can get both?"

"Ah, Americans, yes, of course, a salty sweet couple." I took that to mean food wise. I am not sure what Axel is making of the statement.

We are taken to a tiny table deep down the far end of the room. We pass couples engaged in what seems like serious discussions on world affairs. I am not sure how they can hear each other as the music is loud. I asked the hostess as we walk why it is called the Frog Tooth. She said the owner is eccentric and wanted a couple words that did not go with each other.

Once seated the hostess hands us a menu. The menu print has the same font as that of the scrap of paper we found in Dang's room that said Frog Tooth. Sure enough, on one side are desserts and on the other side are appetizers. At the bottom are listed the Danish microbrews made on premises. A waiter comes by. I give Alex the you take care of this look.

"I'll please have the Lumpfish roe and a bottle of the sweet-spicy Porse Guld and I think Maggie would enjoy the red beetroot ice cream on the bed of black licorice. Oh, and a Porse Guld, too"

The waiter took our menu, smiled and left.

"I would," I asked Axel somewhat shouting to be heard.

"I don't know, but I did not see anything like salmon spread or vanilla bean ice cream."

"I'm just kidding."

"So now what? We are here, Maggie."

"Yes, well, I don't know the next step. But we know now two things for sure. We know that Dang was in Luxembourg and here at the Frog Tooth."

"I think we can be sure he was in Luxembourg because a government document, that is, a boarding pass confirms as much. I hate to be a downer but all we really know is that he used a scrap of paper from this place to jot down the number of his hotel. We don't know that he got the paper here or from a friend of his or...."

Axel suddenly stopped his monologue and stared over my left shoulder. He mouthed the word, "Dang" and his face looked like he was asking, "Dang?"

The waiter arrived with our drinks and I used the opportunity to adjust in my chair and look without looking at what Axel was facing. In the corner I saw a Chinese man laughing it up with a red haired woman who when she turned her face to one side was the woman pictured on his Facebook page. My mind filled with thoughts, including why had I never asked for a picture of Dang? I also had the familiar doubts about my abilities as a detective and as a person for that matter creep back into my feelings. I cleared my mind and fought off the self doubt and focused on what I am looking at which is a young, handsome Chinese man with an expensive suit, big smile and extroverted gestures.

Our food now arrived and we alternated between eating and stealing glances. The red beetroot ice cream was actually good. Axel was eating what looked like fish eggs.

In between fork full, Axel said, "we better do something before they leave and we lose trace of this lead." After marveling at Axel's ease with detective genre parlance, I said, "I'm going over there and execute the plan we had this morning and ask him why he stood me up?"

"I've got your back," Axel said as I stood up.

"Thanks Dano."

I make my way first to the restroom where I wet my hair down and slick it back and open my shirt a bit. I saw Jamie Lee Curtis do this in a movie once. I approach the table.

Dang, if that's him, spots me right away and flashes a teeth full smile, his male instinct kicking in. The red head sees me and gives me a friendly, but get the hell out of here look.

"I was at the Marriott, what happened," I said, deciding to inflame the red head immediately.

"Oh, business, my bad. Maggie this is Bridget, Bridget, Maggie."

I used the introduction to sit down though I had not been invited and started talking, partly out of nerves and partly to gain leads on what might be said back.

"Don't you just love Facebook, it's so social yet completely impersonal. I mean you're networked but still light years apart. Know what I mean? Well, when you no showed I went and looked at art, saw a cool church. I had read that the churches in Europe are empty, except for tourists like me."

"What do you do," Red asked me.

"When I am not busing myself with art, I find things." I thought I noticed Dang's left eye half close slightly.

"Like what," was Red's next question. She was obviously running interference for him.

"Well, most recently I found my neighbor's dog." This made Dang laugh, maybe out of relief so I decided to ratchet up the pressure again. "There's not a lot of money in that so I have moved to finding people. You know, reuniting runaways with their families, that sort of thing."

Dang finished he drink quickly and collect his keys, phone and sunglasses which were all on the table and stood up which caused Red to stand up. "We got to run Maggie, tickets for the concert and we're running late."

"I did not see you look at your watch, but O.K. Bridget, can I friend you?"

"Sure kid, knock yourself out," she said which made me think she probably was not planning on accepting me.

I watched as their backs disappeared and sensed Axel come up beside me.

"Something you said, maybe," Axel asked.

"I think it was when I told them my line of work was finding people."

Case Closed

Last night after the meeting with Dang I sent an e-mail to Dang's parents asking them to scan me a picture of him. This afternoon after it arrived I sent them a reply confirming I had met with their son last night in Copenhagen, but I do not know why he is here or why he is not communicating with them. He looked safe and happy I reported. I asked them to please update Mr. Woo and then I would do the same in person once back in the States.

"I guess I'm done with the case," I said to Axel who was laying in bed reading more on Copenhagen. "But it feels weird like I am not done. There is so much I don't know."

Axel put down the travel book and looked at me. "Your job was to locate him. You did that which I think was remarkable. What he is doing here and why is best left to his family or maybe it's just his right to just do what he pleases. Hey, let me take you out tonight and celebrate your solving your second case. You're rolling. First Terry now Dang."

Primavera

I watch the bartender pour into the shaker centered between Axel and I and our facing stools, Galliano and Campari. Next he cuts two white grapefruits and juices them in with a hand held press, his red fingers and worn cuticles from many years of exposure to citrus turning white as he squeezes. His pencil thin mustache twitching, he strains passion fruit juice carefully over the shaker looking like a mad scientist from the prohibition era with his beaded vest and white apron. Next in is champagne from a bottle he just opened. He caps and shakes with a frenzy to make that loud sound of ice crashing finishing with an expert pour into martini glasses perfectly to each lip not a drop more or less. He pushes them towards us and says, "behold the Primavera or Spring if you don't speak Italian."

Axel proposes a toast as our mixologist watches on beaming with expectation that we will find his creation delightful.

"I thought we would leave the Carlesberg and Tuborg behind tonight and have a proper cocktail. Cheers to my favorite private eye."

We clink and drink.

"Delicious," I say, as Axel closes his eyes smiling and moans with delight after his first swallow. The creator gives a slight bow of the head and leaves us to busy himself washing out glasses behind the bar.

"So what next," Axel asked.

"I don't know," I said.

"I do," he said. "I am in love with the whole Danish eidos."

"What?"

"Eidos is cultural milieu. I have a few places I want to take you while we are here."

"I'm up for it."

"O.K., first we go to Frederiksberg Gardens where there is a statue of Kierkegaard. Then the Royal Library where they have a Kierkegaard archive. Finally, the Copenhagen Museum which has a memorial room about him. I like traveling with you. Let's keep traveling."

"O.K."

We sip our drinks and Axel discusses how Kierkegaard was philosophically very Christian oriented. He remembered reading his book, *Training in Christianity.*

Home

Axel was not kidding when he said we should keep traveling. He surprised me with tickets to China where we went from Copenhagen. He said he wanted me to see the Danish exhibit in Shanghai for the World's Fair. And so I saw the famous mermaid statue in person.

I still cannot believe we are back in Portland now riding our bikes along the Vera Katz Eastbank Esplanade. Axel moved in with me and is finishing his graduate program remotely. Powell's hired him to work in their shipping department. We share rent and expenses. I added him as my domestic partner to the Cobra medical coverage I am still carrying. It is expensive, but I am grateful to be eligible. I have an office at Kate's Espresso and Yoga where she found me some space she was not using so I can grow my detective agency.

End